Dear Parent:

Congratulations! Your child is taking
the first steps on an exciting journey.
The destination? Independent reading!

STEP INTO READING® will help your child get there. The program offers
five steps to reading success. Each step includes fun stories and colorful art.
There are also Step into Reading Sticker Books, Step into Reading Math
Readers, Step into Reading Phonics Readers, Step into Reading Write-In
Readers, and Step into Reading Phonics Boxed Sets—a complete literacy
program with something for every child.

Learning to Read, Step by Step!

Ready to Read   Preschool–Kindergarten
• big type and easy words • rhyme and rhythm • picture clues
For children who know the alphabet and are eager to
begin reading.

Reading with Help   Preschool–Grade 1
• basic vocabulary • short sentences • simple stories
For children who recognize familiar words and sound out
new words with help.

Reading on Your Own   Grades 1–3
• engaging characters • easy-to-follow plots • popular topics
For children who are ready to read on their own.

Reading Paragraphs   Grades 2–3
• challenging vocabulary • short paragraphs • exciting stories
For newly independent readers who read simple sentences
with confidence.

Ready for Chapters   Grades 2–4
• chapters • longer paragraphs • full-color art
For children who want to take the plunge into chapter books
but still like colorful pictures.

STEP INTO READING® is designed to give every child a successful
reading experience. The grade levels are or
through the steps at their own speed, devel
reading, no matter what their grade.

Remember, a lifetime love of reading starts

5
PLAYTIME TALES

Step into Reading, Random House, and the Random House colophon are registered trademarks of
Random House, Inc.

SpongeBob SquarePants created by

Stephen Hillenburg

Visit us on the Web!
StepIntoReading.com
randomhousekids.com

Educators and librarians, for a variety of teaching tools, visit us at RHTeachersLibrarians.com

ISBN 978-0-553-50859-8

MANUFACTURED IN CHINA   10 9 8 7 6 5 4 3 2 1

Random House Children's Books supports the First Amendment and celebrates the right to read.

STEP INTO READING®

5 PLAYTIME TALES

Step 1 and 2 Books

A Collection of Five Early Readers

Random House 🏠 New York

Contents

Dora's Puppy, Perrito!

By Mary Tillworth
Illustrated by Dave Aikins

Random House 🏠 New York

Dora has a puppy.

His name is Perrito.

Dora loves to play
with her puppy!

Dora and Boots
visit Dora's grandmother.

Dora's grandmother
has a gift for Perrito!

Dora says thank you
to her grandmother.

Now Dora and Boots

must get home.

They check Map.

First,
Dora and Boots go
to Butterfly Garden.

Swiper has
a robot butterfly.
He wants to swipe
the gift!

Dora sees Swiper.

"Swiper, no swiping!"

she says.

"Oh, mannn!"
says Swiper.

Dora and Boots

cross a bridge.

The wind blows
the gift away.
The gift flies
into the river!

23

Dora uses a fishing pole.

She hooks the gift!

Dora and Boots

go to the Dancing Trees.

They count the trees.

There are ten!

Dora and Boots

wave their arms.

They look like trees.

They dance the

Tree Dance!

Swiper dresses

like a tree.

He sneaks

past Dora and Boots.

Swiper swipes the gift!

"Swiper, no swiping!
That's Perrito's gift,"
says Dora.

Swiper loves puppies!

He gives the gift back.

Dora and Boots
walk home.
They see Perrito!

The puppy wags his tail.

Dora and Boots open
Perrito's gift.

There is a bowl.

There is a collar.

There is a leash.

There is a bone!

Dora puts
the collar
and the leash
on Perrito.

Perrito chews

on the bone.

He loves it!

Dora loves her puppy!

BiG TRUCK SHOW!

By Mary Tillworth

Based on the teleplay "Humunga-Truck!"
by Rodney Stringfellow

Based on the TV series *Bubble Guppies,*
created by Robert Scull and Jonny Belt

Cover illustrated by Sue DiCicco and Steve Talkowski
Interior illustrated by MJ Illustrations

Random House 🏠 New York

Honk, honk!
Beep, beep!
Here come
the trucks!

A fire truck is red.

It has a ladder.

The siren flashes.

The siren is loud!

A dump truck
is full of sand.

The back goes up.

The sand slides out!

49

A garbage truck
takes trash away.
Pee-yew!

Gil and Molly hold their noses!

A mail truck brings mail.

Goby gets a letter!

Jingle, jingle!
Here comes
the ice cream truck!

Deema eats
a sweet treat.

Oona and Nonny
drive a bread truck.

Bump!
The truck
gets a flat tire.

Oona fixes
the flat tire.

The bread truck
will soon be back
and on a roll!

It is time
for the big truck show!

The crowd
claps and cheers.

There are big trucks.

There are little trucks.

They are very
helpful trucks!

Humunga-Truck
comes out.
It is really big!

Uh-oh!
The big truck
is stuck
in the mud!

Zoom, zoom!
Here comes
the tow truck!

The tow truck
hooks the big truck.

It pulls the big truck
out of the mud!

Hooray for trucks!
Hooray for
Humunga-Truck!

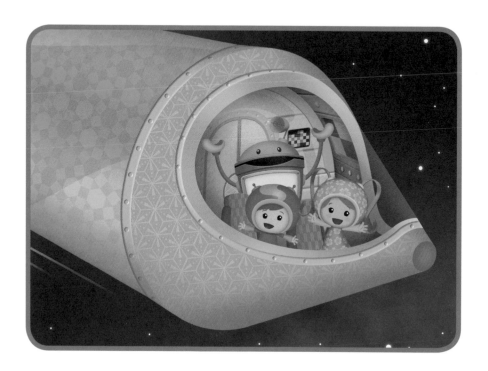

OUTER-SPACE CHASE

Adapted by John Cabell
Based on the original screenplay by Dustin Ferrer
Illustrated by Jason Fruchter

Random House 🏠 New York

Team Umizoomi visits
the Umi City
Space Center.
DoorMouse takes
their tickets.

Milli, Geo, and Bot see
moon rocks and
a space suit.

They also see
a giant rocket!

DoorMouse opens
his lunch box.
His cheese rolls away!

The cheese rolls
onto the rocket.
DoorMouse
chases it.

The rocket blasts off!

DoorMouse is on it!

Team Umizoomi must
save DoorMouse.

It's time for action!

Geo makes a rocket!

Super Shapes!

10, 9, 8, 7, 6,

5, 4, 3, 2, 1.

The rocket takes off!

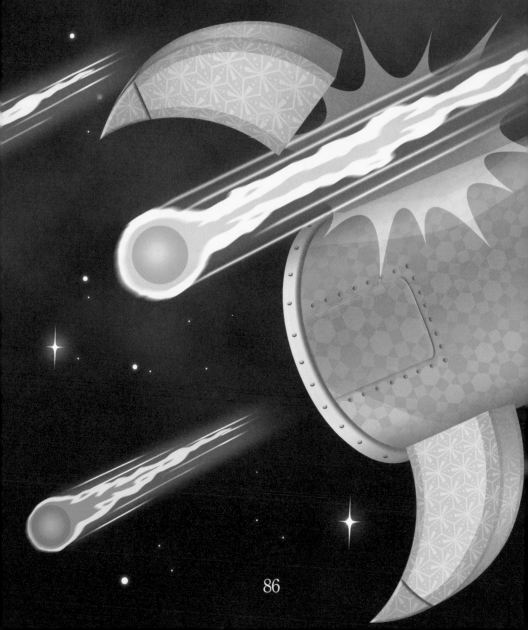

Team Umizoomi

is in space.

Watch out for comets!

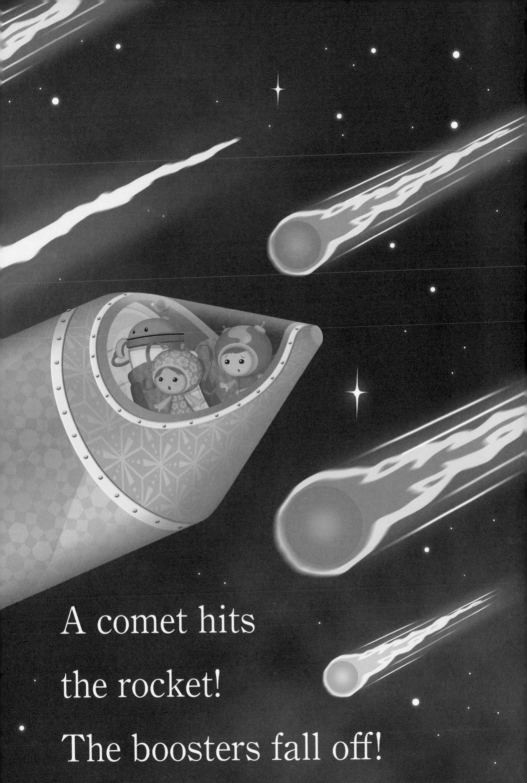

A comet hits
the rocket!
The boosters fall off!

Team Umizoomi looks
for the boosters.
Team Umizoomi meets
an alien.

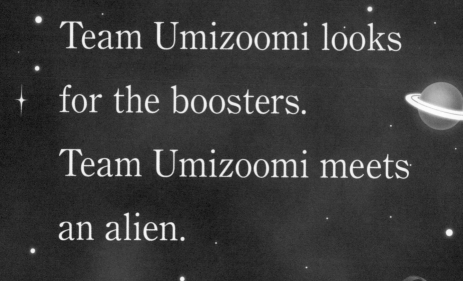

He is wearing
the boosters.
They keep
his feet warm.

Bot gives the
alien some socks.

The alien gives
Bot the boosters.

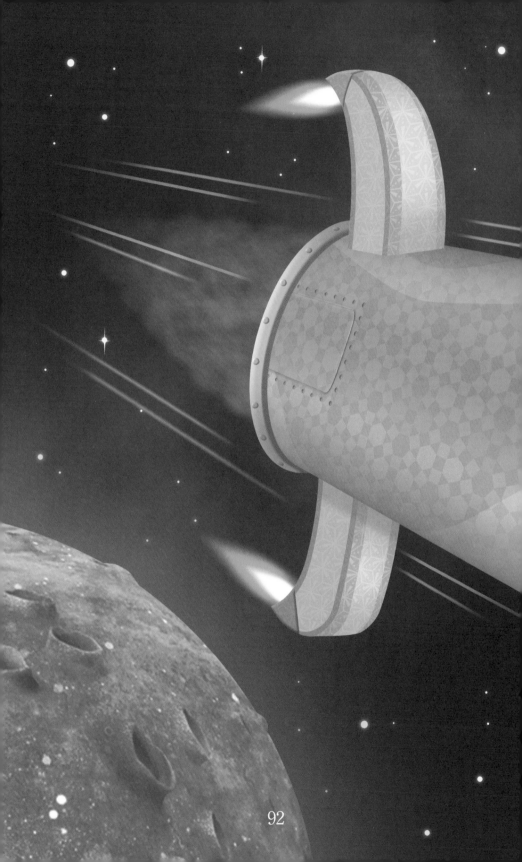

The rocket is fixed!

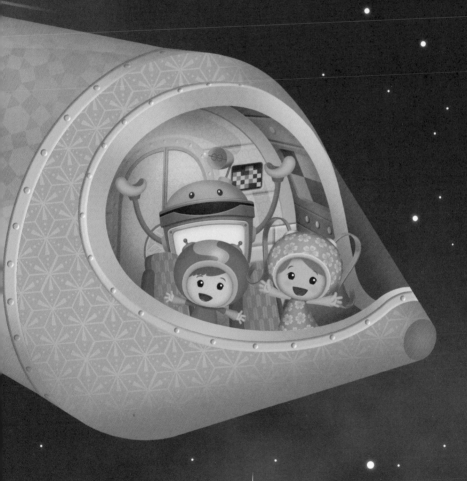

The team must fly
really fast.
They need to find
a Speedy Star.

Milli will find
the Speedy Star.
<u>Pattern Power!</u>

The pattern is
red, yellow, blue.
Milli finds
the Speedy Star!

Team Umizoomi's rocket
flies through the star.
The rocket goes
really fast!

Team Umizoomi finds
DoorMouse's rocket.
It is going to crash
into Mars!

"We need to catch
DoorMouse's rocket!"
says Bot.

Team Umizoomi's rocket
has a Space Magnet.

The Space Magnet catches the rocket!

DoorMouse is
back on Earth!

"We saved DoorMouse!"

says Geo.

2, 4, 6, 8!
Everybody Crazy Shake!

nickelodeon

SPONGEBOB SQUAREPANTS™

Party Time!

By John Cabell
Illustrated by Harry Moore

Random House 🏠 New York

It is
Squidward's birthday!
He gives himself
a new clarinet.

Squidward goes outside.

He plays

his new clarinet.

SpongeBob
is also outside.
He plays fetch
with Gary.

SpongeBob throws
a stick.
"Go get it, Gary!"
he says.

Gary brings
the stick back.
"Meow," says Gary.

Squidward puts
the clarinet down.

Oh, no!
SpongeBob accidentally
grabs the clarinet
and throws it.

Crack!

The clarinet breaks.

"I'm sorry,"
says SpongeBob.

"You have ruined
my birthday!"
yells Squidward.

SpongeBob must fix
Squidward's birthday.
"I will throw him
the best party ever,"
he says.

Patrick will help.
The party will be
at the Krusty Krab.

SpongeBob makes

a delicious cake.

Patrick blows
up balloons
and decorates
the Krusty Krab.

SpongeBob and Patrick make a giant ice statue of Squidward.

SpongeBob wraps
a special gift
for Squidward.
Everything is ready
for the party!

Mr. Krabs goes
to Squidward's house.
Knock, knock!

Squidward opens
the door.
"There is an emergency
at the Krusty Krab!"
says Mr. Krabs.

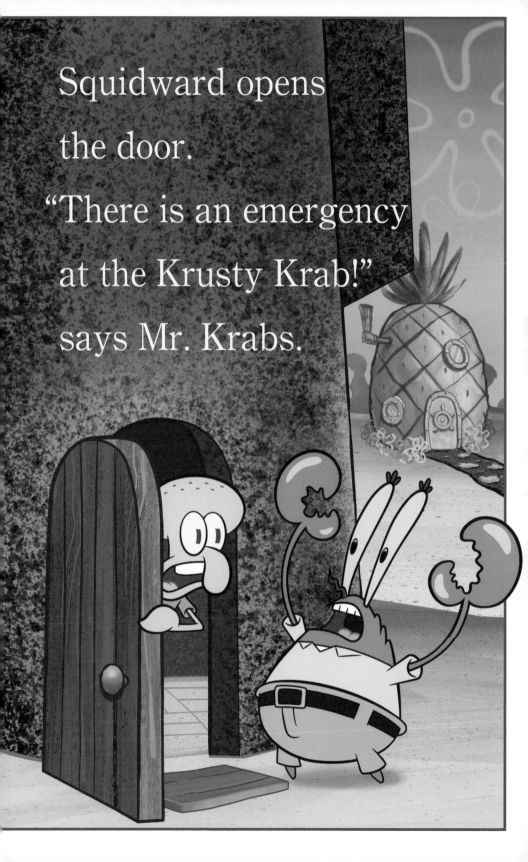

Squidward and Mr. Krabs
run to the Krusty Krab.

When Squidward walks in, everyone cheers. "Surprise!" they shout.

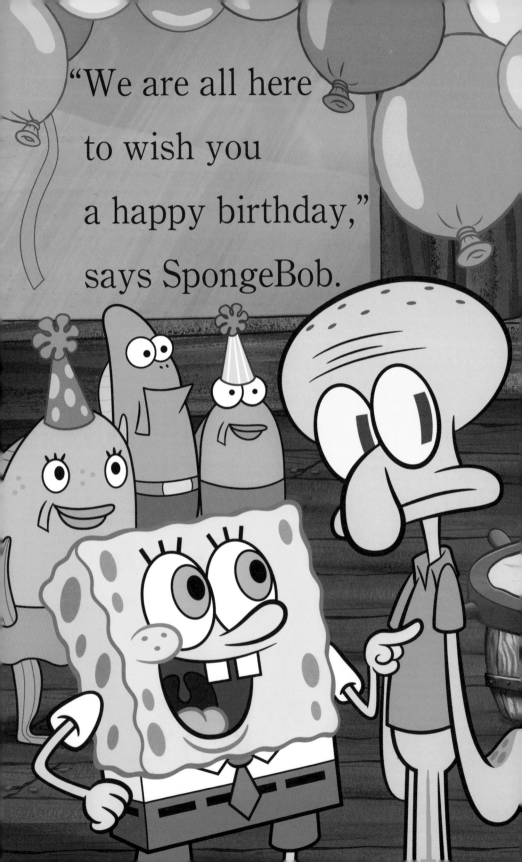

"We are all here to wish you a happy birthday," says SpongeBob.

"I'm here for a Krabby Patty," says a customer.

SpongeBob gives
Squidward a gift.

130

It is

a new clarinet!

Squidward plays
a song.

Hooray!
Everyone claps.
Squidward bows.

Squidward thanks
SpongeBob.
"This was
a great birthday,"
he says.

Happy birthday,
Squidward!

nickelodeon

PAW
PATROL

CHASE IS ON THE CASE!

Based on the teleplay "Pups in a Fog"
by Carolyn Hay
Illustrated by Fabrizio Petrossi

Random House 🏠 New York

Ryder sees a problem
at the lighthouse.

The light is out.
Without it,
ships could crash
into Seal Island!

Captain Turbot calls
Ryder for help.

Captain Turbot cannot
find the lighthouse.
He is lost in the fog!

PAW Patrol is
ready for action!

"We need to fix
the lighthouse,"
Ryder tells the pups.

145

"Chase, I need your searchlight," says Ryder.

"We will need

Zuma's hovercraft, too."

Ryder, Zuma, and Chase
race to Seal Island.

"We have to fix

that light,"

says Ryder.

Wally the walrus
is in the way!
"He wants a treat,"
says Ryder.

He throws a treat.

"Catch, Wally!"

Wally gulps it down.

Ryder, Zuma, and Chase
reach Seal Island.
A big ship is coming!

Chase is
on the case!
He will warn
the ship.

The lighthouse door
is locked!
Chase shoots out
his net.

Ryder climbs up the net.
Now he can go through
the window
and unlock the door.

Chase is in!
He turns on
his searchlight.

The big ship sees
Chase's light.
It turns away
from the rocks.
The ship is safe!

Captain Turbot follows
Chase's light.
He takes a new bulb
to the lighthouse.

The light is bright.

The lighthouse is fixed.

The PAW Patrol has
saved the day!

"Whenever you are in trouble, just yelp for help!" Ryder says.